CLEMENTINE ROSE
and the Bake-Off Dilemma

Jacqueline Harvey

RANDOM HOUSE AUSTRALIA

A Random House book
Published by Penguin Random House Australia Pty Ltd
Level 3, 100 Pacific Highway, North Sydney NSW 2060
penguin.com.au

First published by Random House Australia in 2018

Addresses for the Penguin Random House group of companies can be found at global.penguinrandomhouse.com/offices.

A catalogue record for this book is available from the National Library of Australia

ISBN 978 0 14378 059 5

Cover and internal illustrations by J.Yi
Cover design by Leanne Beattie
Internal design by Midland Typesetters, Australia
Typeset in ITC Century 12.5/19 by Midland Typesetters, Australia
Printed in Australia by Griffin Press, an accredited ISO AS/NZS 14001:2004 Environmental Management System printer

Penguin Random House Australia uses papers that are natural, renewable and recyclable products and made from wood grown in sustainable forests. The logging and manufacturing processes are expected to conform to the environmental regulations of the country of origin.

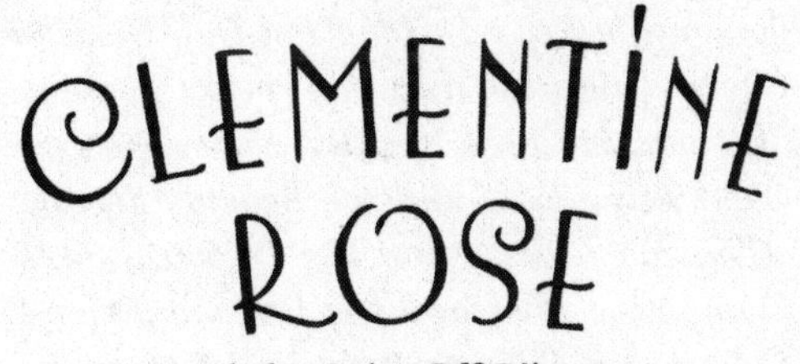

and the Bake-Off Dilemma

Books by Jacqueline Harvey

Clementine Rose and the Surprise Visitor
Clementine Rose and the Pet Day Disaster
Clementine Rose and the Perfect Present
Clementine Rose and the Farm Fiasco
Clementine Rose and the Seaside Escape
Clementine Rose and the Treasure Box
Clementine Rose and the Famous Friend
Clementine Rose and the Ballet Break-In
Clementine Rose and the Movie Magic
Clementine Rose and the Birthday Emergency
Clementine Rose and the Special Promise
Clementine Rose and the Paris Puzzle
Clementine Rose and the Wedding Wobbles
Clementine Rose and the Bake-Off Dilemma

Alice-Miranda at School
Alice-Miranda on Holiday
Alice-Miranda Takes the Lead
Alice-Miranda at Sea
Alice-Miranda in New York
Alice-Miranda Shows the Way
Alice-Miranda in Paris
Alice-Miranda Shines Bright
Alice-Miranda in Japan
Alice-Miranda at Camp
Alice-Miranda at the Palace
Alice-Miranda in the Alps
Alice-Miranda to the Rescue
Alice-Miranda in China
Alice-Miranda Holds the Key
Alice-Miranda in Hollywood
Alice-Miranda in Scotland

Kensy and Max: Breaking News
Kensy and Max: Disappearing Act

For my mum, Jennifer, who makes
the best devil's food cake ever

FLOP

Clementine Rose climbed onto the kitchen stool as her mother pulled the round tin from the oven and placed it on the bench in front of her. She leaned over and breathed in the delicious aroma, impatient for the cake to cool down so she could decorate it. She had already helped to whip the cream and cut the strawberries and had planned to arrange them in a pretty pattern.

'It's perfect,' she said, sighing happily. Then watched in horror as the centre of the cake collapsed like a sinkhole. 'Uh-oh.'

Lady Clarissa spun around and caught sight of the crater. 'Oh heavens, that wasn't supposed to happen,' she said with a frown. 'I must have forgotten to add the baking powder. Honestly, my brain has been a sieve lately.'

Clementine could only agree. Her mother had been forgetting a lot of things. Last Saturday, she had left poor Aunt Violet stranded at the train station in the rain for an hour. On Monday, she had sent Clementine off to school with an empty lunch box and had returned from Mrs Mogg's shop with a loaf of bread and a jar of peanut butter. It wouldn't have been so peculiar if Clarissa hadn't made the trip especially for eggs and milk. She was even late collecting Clementine from her ballet class this afternoon.

Clarissa wiped down the bench and rinsed the cloth, then emptied the contents of the cake tin into Lavender's bowl.

'You haven't forgotten it's half-term holidays soon, have you, Mummy?' Clementine asked through a mouthful of strawberries.

After the busyness of the last few months, Clarissa and Drew had promised the children a trip to the city. Clementine had been counting down the days on the kitchen calendar and now there was only a week left of school. She couldn't wait for all the activities they'd planned. There was to be a visit to the ballet, a picnic at the Bauers' farm as well as sleepovers, games and baking galore. Aunt Violet and Uncle Digby had promised to take her and Will to the museum too.

Violet Appleby appeared at the bottom of the kitchen stairs looking very stylish in a navy pants-suit and cream silk blouse. 'Something smells good,' she said, wandering over to put the kettle on. The old woman turned to retrieve a teacup from the cupboard and spotted the disaster in Lavender's bowl. 'Godfathers! What happened to that?'

'It's a flop,' Clementine said, hopping off the stool. She disappeared into the pantry with her pet pig, Lavender, trailing after her.

'I forgot the baking powder,' Clarissa explained, shaking her head. She closed the recipe book and discovered she had propped it up using the missing ingredient.

'We can have the chocolate brownies that Uncle Digby helped me make yesterday,' Clementine suggested, emerging from the pantry with a large tin in her arms. She placed it on the kitchen table and opened the lid. 'Would you like one, Aunt Violet?'

The old woman arched an eyebrow. 'What did you call me?'

'Oops!' Clementine's eyes widened. 'It's hard to remember sometimes because you're everyone's Aunt Violet and you're only *my* granny,' she said, then wondered whether that meant her head was a sieve too. She gave it a little shake, but it felt the same as usual.

Violet Appleby's features softened. 'I suppose I'm still getting used to *being* a granny,'

she said, and held out her arms for a quick cuddle.

It was only a couple of months ago that Clementine had learned that her great-aunt Violet's daughter, Eliza, was her biological mother. Upon discovering she was dreadfully ill with no hope of recovery, Eliza left her daughter in the care of the person she trusted most in the world – her cousin Lady Clarissa Appleby. She pinned a letter to the baby's blanket and placed Clementine in a basket of dinner rolls in the back of Pierre Rousseau's van, just before it puttered its way to Penberthy House. Since that fateful day, Clarissa had raised the child as her own and had never once looked back. She loved Clementine with all her heart and, like anyone who knew the charming little girl, couldn't imagine life without her. This news, of course, meant that Clementine's great-aunt Violet wasn't her great-aunt at all, but her grandmother.

Clarissa wiped her forehead with the back of her hand. There was no time for another cake now. She had to make a start on dinner as two guests were due to arrive shortly and they had requested the full service.

'How many do we have staying tonight?' Aunt Violet asked. She finished pouring herself a cup of tea and took a brownie from the tin.

Clementine performed a series of jetés towards the reservations book beside the telephone. She ran her finger down the page until it landed on Friday. 'Only two. Mr and Mrs Loveberry.'

Aunt Violet's forehead puckered. 'Where have I heard that name before? Perhaps on the television . . .'

Clementine's eyes lit up. 'Do you think our guests are famous like Miss Wells?' she asked. Agnes Wells was her favourite author and had once stayed at Penberthy House while writing a new book. Clementine twirled on the spot and leaned forward into arabesque, the way Ana Hobbs had taught her class an hour earlier.

'Who's famous?' Drew asked, tramping through the back door with Will in tow. They'd been at a school soccer tournament in Downsfordvale, a good couple of hours' drive away. By the looks of it, the boy had taken a few tumbles on the muddy field. He was sporting a grazed knee and a shiny silver medallion around his neck.

'Mr and Mrs Loveberry,' Clementine answered, skipping over to admire her stepbrother's winnings. 'It's so shiny!' she marvelled.

Will grinned and handed the medal to her for closer inspection. 'We came second,' he said proudly. Spotting the open biscuit tin, he rewarded himself with the largest brownie from the centre. 'We lost the final by one goal in extra time, but there were twenty teams and the kids who beat us were really good.'

'You didn't mention the Loveberrys were coming, Clarissa,' Drew said, his face draining of all its colour. 'That can't be right. Not today.'

Clarissa bit her lip, hoping she hadn't forgotten something important. 'Do we know the Loveberrys?'

Drew looked at her in bewilderment. 'Basil and I have been talking to Florence and Nobby Loveberry about filming their new show here, in Penberthy Floss. Don't you remember me telling you?'

'Oh, *of course*!' Aunt Violet exclaimed, startling the sphynx cat that had settled on her lap. Pharaoh jumped to the ground and skittered out of the room. 'Nobby Loveberry and his wife are famous for their bakery, Loveberry's. It has been in the family for hundreds of years. One of Nobby's ancestors invented the Loveberry Bun. It's like nothing you've ever tasted – light as a cloud, sweet but not too sweet, fluffy and bread-like all at once. And, before you say brioche, I can assure you it is far superior.'

Clementine thought that sounded magical. She hoped the Loveberrys travelled with their famous buns.

Drew nodded. 'They're coming to see if we're up to scratch, and I've heard rumours the wife can be tricky. There's no one else staying for the weekend, is there, Clarissa? I know they wanted to keep the whole project confidential until the final decision was made.'

Clarissa pressed her forefinger against her lip. 'No, it's just them, and I do remember now. If they decide to film here, we'll stand to make more money in those couple of weeks than in six months of regular trade. Oh, I'm so sorry, darling. I think I must be losing my mind.'

Drew walked over and squeezed his wife's shoulder. 'Of course you're not, and I didn't mean to bark. It's just that, if we get the job, we might be able to afford that special holiday we've been talking about.'

At the mention of a holiday, Clementine and Will looked at each other and grinned.

Digby Pertwhistle walked in through the swinging door, humming a cheerful tune.

'The Sage Room is all ready, Clarissa,' he said with a sparkle in his voice.

'I hate to overstep the mark here, but I'm afraid that won't do at all,' Drew said. 'We must put the Loveberrys in the Rose Room.'

The old butler's eyebrows jumped up. 'Is that really necessary? I've stripped the sheets and pulled all the furniture away from the walls to clean the skirting boards tomorrow. It's a frightful mess in there.'

Clementine executed a slightly wonky pirouette as the doorbell sounded. All eyes turned towards the entrance.

'Right,' Drew said, leaping into action. 'Digby, you and I will whip the Rose Room into shape. Aunt Violet, you're on charm offensive. Clarissa, can you serve tea and cake in the sitting room? I'll be down as quick as I can to give you a hand.'

'About that cake . . .' Clarissa glanced at Lavender's bowl, where the little pig was making short work of the mangled lump.

Drew winced. 'Oh dear, that's a problem.'

'We can serve my brownies?' Clementine offered.

Will, who was licking his fingers one by one, froze and his eyes grew to the size of saucers. Clementine peered into the tin. Somehow the boy had managed to polish off six brownies in the past ten minutes and now there were none left. Will hid his hands behind his back and cast his eyes to the ground.

'Sorry, Dad,' he mumbled. 'I was starving.'

Drew closed his eyes and thought for a moment. 'Not to worry. It's easily fixed,' the man said. 'How about you and Clemmie run along to Mrs Mogg's shop and see if she has one of Pierre's cakes? Just make sure you bring it home in one piece.'

Will nodded. 'I've still got my soccer boots on, so I'll be super fast,' he promised.

'Even though you know you should have taken them off at the back door,' Aunt Violet said, over the rim of her teacup.

Chastened, Will blushed and accepted the notes Clarissa handed him from her purse.

'Tell Mrs Mogg I'll pay her the rest tomorrow if it's not enough,' the woman instructed, 'and please be careful crossing the road, you two. Don't forget to look left and right.'

'We will,' the children chorused.

The doorbell rang again, and the family dispersed to attend to their tasks. Without a moment to lose, Clementine took Will's hand in hers and the pair shot off out the back door.

SPLAT!

Clementine and Will ran as quickly as they could through the back garden and across the field, past the church and over the road to the village shop. Mrs Mogg's old tabby cat, Claws, was sunning himself on the bench seat on the veranda. He opened one eye as the children charged through the door with the tinkly bell.

'Hello!' Clementine called loudly, gasping for breath. She spied one of Pierre's strawberry sponge cakes sitting under the domed stand on the counter, but Mrs Mogg was nowhere to be seen.

'What should we do?' Will asked. He didn't like the idea of just taking the cake, but maybe they could write a note and leave the money.

'Why don't you get the cake and I'll fetch Mrs Mogg from the house?' Clementine suggested. She pointed to one of the shelves that lined the back wall. 'The boxes are just there, but you'll have to put it together yourself.'

'We made cubes from scratch in Maths last week, so I think I can do it,' Will said. He darted around to the other side of the counter.

Clementine continued on through the door that linked the shop to the Moggs' home and surveyed the sitting room. There was nothing out of the ordinary. The newspaper was open on the coffee table, the cushions were neatly arranged on the couch and the aroma of a freshly baked cake hung in the air. If she wasn't worried before, she was now. Mrs Mogg would never leave the shop unattended.

Clementine checked the rest of the house. She even knocked on the bathroom door, but it was clear there was no one home. She was about to turn back when she heard a faint noise. It sounded like tapping, but she couldn't work out where it was coming from. Then she remembered the shed out the back, which Mrs Mogg used to store items for the shop. Clementine raced through the utility room and out into the garden, where the tapping became banging.

'Help!' came a muffled cry. 'Help me, please!'

Clementine turned the key in the lock and pulled open the shed door. Margaret Mogg stumbled out, her hair dishevelled and her stockings laddered. Judging by the makeshift tower of boxes and crates inside, the woman had been trying to climb high enough to reach the window.

'Thank goodness you're here, Clemmie,' the woman gasped, embracing the girl. 'I thought I was going to be stuck in there until tomorrow evening as Mr Mogg's visiting his brother for the night. I ducked out to fetch a couple of bottles of olive oil and the wind blew the door shut. That was at least an hour ago.'

'It wouldn't have been a very nice place to sleep,' Clementine agreed. The storage shed looked like just the place for lots of creepy-crawlies.

Back inside the shop, Will was balancing the cake on a spatula when he heard the bell. He looked up and was surprised to see Mrs Bottomley, the cranky Kindergarten teacher from their school.

'And what do you think you're doing, young man?' the woman barked, striding towards him.

If he didn't know better, Will could have sworn her hair threw out electric sparks. The lad jumped in fright, sending the cake soaring into the air, over the counter and right onto Mrs Bottomley's ample chest. Will's mouth formed a perfect circle as great chunks of strawberry sponge fell down the woman's front, grazing her skirt and landing with a *splat* on her sturdy brown shoes.

'You dreadful boy!' Ethel screeched. 'You did that on purpose!'

'I . . . I swear I didn't mean to,' Will stuttered. He grabbed a handful of tissues from the box on the counter and tried to pass them to Mrs Bottomley, who batted them away.

Meanwhile, Clementine had brought Mrs Mogg up to speed on their urgent business. The two stepped into the shop and were stunned by the scene in front of them. Clementine could feel a giggle bubbling up inside her and clamped her mouth with both hands.

'I didn't mean it,' Will said with pleading eyes. 'Mrs Bottomley growled at me and I lost control of the cake.'

'I did no such thing,' the teacher muttered, grumpily dabbing at a jam stain on her beige

blouse. 'You'll never hear me growling at a child. What a nonsense.'

That was a big fat lie if Clementine had ever heard one. Mrs Bottomley was *always* growling at children – everyone knew that.

Margaret Mogg bustled forward. 'I'm sure it was an accident,' she said, handing Ethel a clean tea towel from behind the counter. 'Now, we must find you two something for afternoon tea.'

'But that was your only cake,' Will said miserably. He had just wanted to help his father and now he'd ruined everything.

'Well, it must be your lucky day because I made a passionfruit sponge this morning and it's out the back,' Mrs Mogg said with a wink. 'We can't allow Florence and Nobby Loveberry to starve, now, can we?'

Ethel Bottomley's eyes shot up from where she was attempting to remove the cream from her tummy. 'The Loveberrys! They're *here*?' she squeaked, quaking with excitement. She grabbed the tissues from Will and began to fan herself. 'I just *adore* them. Their last cooking show was the best thing I'd seen in years! Are they filming it again?'

Clementine nodded. 'They're staying at the hotel for the weekend and they're thinking of filming their new show here in Penberthy Floss. If they do, Mummy and Drew are going to make lots of money and take us all on a holiday,' she said, earning herself a dig in the ribs from Will.

'It's meant to be a secret, remember?' he whispered.

For the second time in as many minutes, Clementine's hands flew to her mouth. 'Oops!'

'Don't worry, your secret is safe with us,' Mrs Mogg said with a smile. 'Isn't that right, Ethel?' She looked over at Mrs Bottomley, but the woman was already heading for the exit. 'Oh dear, children, I think our chances of keeping that news quiet might have just walked out the door.'

THE LOVEBERRYS

'This cake looks delicious,' Clarissa said as she whipped off her apron and picked up the fully laden tea tray.

Clementine knelt down on the floor to give Lavender a tickle. 'Would you like us to help?' she asked.

'Thank you, darling, but I'd rather you and Will stay here with the animals and make sure that no one does a disappearing act.' Clarissa smiled at the girl. 'The last thing we need is an unexpected visit from Lavender or Pharaoh.'

Given her track record of spilling things on guests, Clementine thought her mother was probably right.

Clarissa reached the swinging door and was just about to push it open when she suddenly felt violently ill. 'Oh dear,' she gasped, turning a peaky shade of green. She placed the tray onto the sideboard and dashed out into the hall, presumably heading for the downstairs powder room.

Will and Clementine looked at one another and then at the tray.

'You take that side and I'll get the other,' Will said.

Clementine nodded. 'We mustn't spill a drop.'

The children might as well have been carrying the Queen's own supper as they marched down the hallway, across the foyer and into the sitting room with the sombre concentration of foot soldiers. Florence and Nobby Loveberry were seated beside one another on the sofa facing the front windows while Aunt Violet was perched in a wing-backed armchair. She was chortling loudly at something Mr Loveberry had said when she caught sight of the children and frowned, wondering what had happened to Clarissa. Having a mud-splattered boy and a six-year-old ballerina serve afternoon tea was hardly the tone they were hoping to set.

Mrs Loveberry sniffed. '*Finally.* I was beginning to think you were milling the flour and fetching the tea leaves from Sri Lanka,' she said, tittering in a way that set Violet's teeth on edge.

The children put down the tray and breathed a sigh of relief just as a loud thud sounded overhead. Florence Loveberry's eyes turned towards the ceiling.

'Goodness me!' she exclaimed. 'Is there a wild animal on the loose?'

'Oh no, the animals are in the kitchen and

they're not wild,' Clementine assured her. 'Unless Mummy's cooking boiled cabbage – that makes Lavender a bit crazy, but only because she loves it so much.'

'Don't worry, Lavender doesn't bite,' Will added, spotting the alarm on the woman's already pinched face. 'And even though Pharaoh looks like an alien, he's really a pussycat.'

Violet Appleby glared at Will for casting aspersions on her precious boy. She wondered again where Clarissa had got to. Things were taking a turn for the worse. But she needn't have worried, as Mr Loveberry found the children to be perfectly charming.

'How fascinating!' he said, sitting forward. 'I can't wait to meet them. You know, I once had a pet tiger myself. My mother insisted he was just a large tabby cat, but I knew better.' He tapped the side of his nose and grinned knowingly.

Clementine grinned back. She decided she liked Mr Loveberry very much, and she liked him even more when Will pointed out that the man's socks were patterned with hundreds and thousands.

Mrs Loveberry rolled her eyes. While her husband was a jolly fellow who smiled all the time, even when he didn't mean to, she wore a cold expression and far too many pearls. The woman was practically covered in them. They dangled from her ears, hung in strands around her neck, dotted the buttons of her cashmere cardigan, adorned her velvet headband and were stuck fast to the buckles of her pink suede shoes. Florence Loveberry clearly wasn't a fan of the idea that less is more.

Clementine noticed the woman had a notebook on her lap and a fountain pen too. It reminded her of the time she had borrowed a similar pen from her grandfather's desk, thinking it would help make her writing fancy. Instead, it had made an awful inky mess all over her mother's bedspread. Mrs Loveberry opened her notebook and quickly wrote something inside, then snapped it shut again.

Violet set about pouring the tea while Mr Loveberry cut the cake. He picked up a slice and fanned the aroma towards him. At one point it seemed as though he was about to plunge his nose right into the middle of the sponge, but he stopped short and inhaled deeply.

'There's a secret ingredient I can't quite put my finger on,' he said, passing the plate to his wife, who set about mimicking the same routine.

The woman closed her eyes and brought the plate up to the tip of her nose. She then took a bite and chewed it for what felt like an eternity. Clementine was beginning to wilt with anticipation. 'Elderflower,' Mrs Loveberry said after a long pause. 'Passionfruit and elderflower – the flavour of the moment. A little clichéd perhaps, but the combination certainly works.'

The doorbell rang.

'I'll get it,' Clementine said, and raced out to the front foyer with Will hot on her heels.

Not a minute later, Ethel Bottomley bustled into the room, cake-free and with her tight brown curls piled high. It looked as if a giant brown shrub was sitting on her head. Clementine and Will had tried their best to stop the woman, but she had been most insistent.

Violet Appleby looked up in surprise. Ethel was never one to drop by unannounced – unless, of course, she was here to snoop. Judging by the look on her face, *that* was absolutely the case. Violet stared daggers at the woman, then turned to the Loveberrys with a smile plastered across her face. 'Excuse me a moment while I speak with Mrs Bottomley outside.'

'But we haven't even been introduced,' Ethel protested.

The Loveberrys were completely oblivious, having each taken a bite of the passionfruit sponge. Nobby licked his lips while Florence popped another large chunk of cake into her mouth.

'Whoever baked this has to be on the show,' Nobby declared.

His wife nodded, dabbing at the corners of her pursed lips with a napkin. 'I completely agree.'

Clementine gasped and jiggled on the spot. She couldn't wait to tell Mrs Mogg. The woman would be thrilled!

'It was me! I baked that cake!' Mrs Bottomley blurted, yelling so loudly that Mrs Loveberry almost dropped her plate.

'No, you didn't,' Will said, frowning. 'Mrs Mogg did.'

'Yes, and she should really be on your show,' Clementine added.

The Loveberrys exchanged curious glances. 'Well, we will keep that in mind,' Florence said, gathering up her notebook and pen. 'I think we have seen enough here.'

Clementine's eyes widened in horror. 'Please don't go,' she begged. 'I didn't mean to tell Mrs Bottomley that you were here. I only told Mrs Mogg when we went to fetch the cake because it was an emergency.'

Drew and Uncle Digby stepped into the room, having finally finished getting everything ready upstairs. 'Oh, hello Mr Loveberry, Mrs Loveberry,' Drew said, casting a sideways glance at Ethel and wondering what she was doing there. 'My apologies for the delay. I hope you've enjoyed your afternoon tea.'

Florence Loveberry smirked. 'I'm not sure if *enjoyed* is quite the word I'd use,' she said, tittering again.

'Yes, well, we'd best be off then,' Nobby said, rising to his feet. 'You see, I've reached an age where, unless I have a kip before dinner, I'll be sound asleep at the table by seven.'

'So, you're not leaving?' Clementine asked.

Florence Loveberry peered down her pointy nose at the child. 'Of course not. If we're going to start filming in another week, there is much to be done.'

Clementine's heart sank. 'But that's the holidays,' she murmured. Uncle Digby put an arm around her and whispered that she shouldn't worry. They would still have plenty of time to do lots of fun things.

'When did you decide?' Drew asked the Loveberrys. 'I thought you were only here to inspect us.'

Nobby looked at him with a quizzical smile. 'I spoke to your wife yesterday. I thought she might have relayed the news, but she seemed rather preoccupied.'

Clementine glanced at Will, who looked at Drew, who turned to Digby, who shrugged at Aunt Violet, who eyed the door. There was certainly something strange going on with Clarissa. This wasn't like her at all.

'Well, I'm thrilled,' Drew said, smiling with his teeth. 'And I can promise you that setting *The Great Village Bake-Off* here in Penberthy Floss is going to be the best decision you have ever made. This show will be your finest yet.'

A smile settled on Florence Loveberry's lips, but it held none of her husband's warmth. 'Yes,' she said, 'I certainly hope you're right about that.'

HUNDREDS AND THOUSANDS

Auditions for *The Great Village Bake-Off* were to be held on Sunday at the village hall. A queue could be seen snaking along the veranda, all the way past Mrs Mogg's shop and around the end of the road. There were even more people than when the hall was reopened after the fire, and that had been a very special occasion with the mayor presiding over the event. Clementine was surprised to see her classmate Joshua Tribble among them, holding a large cake box.

'There must be hundreds and thousands of people,' Clementine said.

'I think you mean hundreds *of* thousands, Clementine, and I suspect that's well over-stating the fact,' Aunt Violet pointed out.

Clementine stared up at the old woman and wrinkled her nose. One thing that hadn't changed since finding out Aunt Violet was her grandmother was the number of times the woman corrected her.

She and Will followed Aunt Violet through the side door and into the building. Drew and Basil had been there for hours already with their crew. They were filming every audition so the Loveberrys could remember each entrant and see what they were like on camera. Basil was directing the production and Drew was in charge of sound, but there were at least five other crew members behind cameras and operating computers. Clementine was disappointed that her mother hadn't joined them this morning. Clarissa still wasn't feeling well, which was very strange as she rarely even caught a cold.

Clementine spotted Pierre Rousseau, her best friend Sophie's father. He was hard to miss, dressed as he was in his white baker's uniform and tall hat. Drew had told her Pierre was going to decide the winner in the grand finale and they were filming a few shots of him for the promotional advertisements this morning.

'*Bonjour* Pierre!' she called, waving to him.

Pierre looked over and broke into a grin. '*Bonjour* Clementine!' he replied, waving back.

Nearby, Florence Loveberry was fluffing her hair in front of a large mirror. Clementine noticed that the woman's notebook was sitting on the table in front of her. She thought it must be very important to be carried around everywhere. Clementine wondered if the woman took it to the toilet with her the way Uncle Digby took the newspaper in with him every morning.

'Nobby, where on earth is Susan?' Mrs Loveberry demanded. 'Really, I think we need to consider getting a new personal assistant – she is terribly unreliable these days.' The woman pressed the nozzle on the tin of hairspray, enveloping everyone within twenty metres in a cloud of sticky mist.

Clementine's eyes watered and she turned to cough into her hand.

Nobby Loveberry chuckled. 'Now, now, dear, it wouldn't be right to sack our own daughter. She does have four children to look after.' The man's phone rang and he pulled it out of his pocket. 'Hello Susan, we were just . . . Oh heavens,' he said, his eyebrows furrowing. 'Not to worry, we'll make do. Of course you should. Take care and give our love to the children.' He hung up the phone and looked at his wife, who had swivelled around in her chair.

'What is it this time?' she barked.

'I'm afraid Harry's come down with a fever and Brian's had to take the rest of them to watch Cleo's ballet concert,' Nobby replied with a smile. 'At least the other children will get to see their sister perform.'

Florence rolled her eyes. 'How are we meant to do all the administration and film the auditions at the same time? *I'm* certainly not checking off names. You'll need to find someone to replace her and quick smart. Really, Nobby, she might be our daughter, but her priorities are all over the place. She could have arranged a babysitter.'

Violet sighed inwardly. She couldn't leave Drew and Basil in the lurch – this production meant a lot to the both of them. 'I can step in if you need someone at the last minute,' she offered.

'Will and I could help too,' Clementine piped up. 'We didn't spill your tea the other day.'

Nobby Loveberry's grin reached from ear to ear. 'Well, that is a wonderful offer and we would be very happy to accept. Thank you.'

At quarter to ten, Basil opened the front doors. Each entrant was to register with

Violet Appleby, record a piece to camera and have their photograph taken by Will. They would then be escorted to meet the Loveberrys, who would sample a bite of their cake. Will and Clementine quickly took their places and waited for the first entrant.

'I want to be Mr Loveberry when I grow up,' Will whispered. 'Imagine getting paid to eat cake all day.'

'You'd probably get a tummy ache,' Clementine whispered back.

The first person through the door was a portly fellow called Serge Moreno. He had a dark moustache and thick black hair and could barely keep hold of his cake he was trembling so much.

'Good morning,' Clementine said with a smile. 'That's a beautiful cake – is it a croquembouche?'

If the man hadn't been so nervous, he might have wondered how a six-year-old had come to know of such a dish. 'Hello,' he whispered with a small nod, then gasped loudly when he caught sight of the Loveberrys. It took several minutes to get the information they needed as the man was unable to speak.

'Godfathers,' Aunt Violet muttered once he'd gone, 'I hope they're all not as overwhelmed as Mr Moreno or we'll be here until midnight.'

But with Clementine greeting everyone at the door, the queue began to move at a steady pace. The child had a knack for putting people at ease and there certainly were a lot of them. It seemed that everyone who lived within a hundred miles of Penberthy Floss had come to throw their hat into the ring. Clementine thought Mrs Bottomley had done a very good job of spreading the news in just one day. She was surprised by how many children were there too. Clementine loved baking and had been practising a lot lately, but she had been sorely disappointed to discover that contestants for the show had to be sixteen years or older. It hardly seemed fair. She would have loved to try out.

All in all, there were a few cakes she hoped tasted better than they looked, but they were mostly lovely. Several of them appeared questionably similar to the cakes from Pierre's Patisserie. It must have been a strange coincidence, too, that there were a few people who turned on their heels and fled the building upon spotting Pierre in the hall.

There was one lady in particular who captured Clementine's attention. Her name was Tiggy Edwards and she was a florist from Briar Meadow, a village fifty miles away. Clementine loved her outfit, which consisted of a gorgeous floral dress with a full skirt and a little cardigan over the top with matching baby blue kitten heels. Clementine thought she looked like one of those old-fashioned movie stars from the films Aunt Violet enjoyed watching on rainy days. Miss Edwards spoke in soft tones and giggled nervously every now and then. Her cake was delicately wrapped in an emerald fondant

and decorated with edible flowers, candied fruit and spun sugar. It resembled an English rose garden in summer. Clementine could hardly believe the flowers weren't real, they were so lifelike.

It was just before the lunch break when a fellow called Ernest Biggins was called for his turn. The man had a bushy beard and wore a pork-pie hat and thick glasses with a long overcoat and shoes that looked too big. Clementine noticed he had a rather strange and cumbersome way of walking, and wondered about the state of his beard, which seemed to be separating from the side of his face. He shuffled forward and presented a giant layered peach creation.

Intrigued, Clementine inched forward to take a closer look. When Mr Biggins answered one of Mr Loveberry's questions, the girl's eyes bulged. She tapped Will on the shoulder and whispered in his ear. The pair of them began to giggle behind their hands, earning a stern look from Drew.

Florence Loveberry turned and glared at the children. 'What's the matter with you two?' she squawked.

'That's not Mr Biggins, that's Mrs Bottomley,' Clementine blurted.

'Nonsense!' the man squeaked. Then, as if remembering himself, repeated the phrase two octaves lower.

Violet Appleby glanced up from her paperwork and was startled to see Mrs Loveberry march up to the man and pull hard on his beard. To her great shock, it came away in the woman's hand. 'Heavens, Ethel,' Violet tutted, 'that was a jolly good disguise and you might have got away with it if Clementine hadn't noticed.'

'Well, I'm very disappointed, Mrs Bottomley, because this cake is outstanding,' Nobby said with a sympathetic smile. 'What do you think, Pierre? Children, take a piece for yourselves.'

Pierre smacked his lips appreciatively. '*Delicieux*.'

'Nisyum,' Will mumbled with his mouth full.

Clementine nodded vigorously. She could only agree and she wasn't the biggest fan of peaches.

Florence Loveberry was in raptures. 'If only you hadn't tried to pass off Margaret Mogg's cake as your own the other day, you could still be in the race,' she said, shaking her head and scribbling in her notebook.

'But I actually baked this cake,' Ethel protested. 'I didn't think you'd let me audition because of the other afternoon when I told a small untruth about that passionfruit sponge.' Ethel Bottomley sniffled and wrung the pork-pie hat in her hands. 'If only you'd let me prove it.'

Clementine thought it was a bit harsh that one little white lie meant the woman couldn't even try out. 'Mrs Bottomley could make another cake right here in the hall kitchen,' the girl suggested. 'Then you'd know for sure.'

The Loveberrys looked at one another and then at Pierre, who shrugged his shoulders. Nobby agreed it would be a shame to disqualify Mrs Bottomley if indeed it was her cake, especially as it was one of the best he'd tasted so far.

'I could supervise,' Pierre offered. 'I will not let Mrs Bottomley out of my sight.'

'You wouldn't mind?' Nobby asked.

'*Au contraire*, I am 'appy to 'elp.' Pierre turned to Mrs Bottomley. ''Ow long will it take for you to gather the ingredients?'

'Brilliant!' the woman fizzed. 'I have everything in the car.' Mrs Bottomley raced outside as fast as her oversized shoes could carry her.

PIECE OF CAKE

It was mid-afternoon when Odette Rousseau arrived at the hall with Sophie and Jules. The woman offered to stand in for Clementine and Will so the children could all go outside and enjoy the sunshine for a while. The foursome was swiftly joined by Joshua and Astrid, and Tilda and Teddy Hobbs. Soon enough a vigorous game of soccer was underway in the churchyard, with Father Bob donating a ball to the cause and constructing makeshift goalposts, although the man was unable to referee due to a fundraising meeting scheduled with some parishioners.

Joshua was in a terrible mood, having been told that only his mother would be able to try out for the bake-off. He wasn't the only one.

'Grown-ups aren't always better than children,' Astrid declared, and the rest of them agreed. The girl was well qualified to say so, too, given the fact she had beaten Mr Smee at the spelling bee earlier in the term.

Unfortunately, Joshua's competitive side was about to get the better of him. The lad not only decreed that the teams would be divided between girls and boys, but he then set about yelling that girls were hopeless. After a terse exchange of words with Clementine and her friends, the boy's bad mood was made worse when the girls' team scored the first two goals. While the boys fought back to level the score, the game ended in disaster with Joshua barrelling up the field, kicking Clementine in the shins, then pushing Sophie flat on her back and booting the ball into the goal via Astrid's face.

'Woohoo!' he cried, leaping about. 'We win!'

Will, Jules, Tilda and Teddy abandoned the game to attend to their friends. Clementine was holding back tears and rubbing her shin. 'Why do you always have to be so mean, Joshua?' she yelled.

Thankfully, the boy's mother was calling to him.

'Girls are *losers*,' Joshua spat, and poked out his tongue before running off.

Mr Mogg had been taking a break outside the front of the shop and witnessed the lad's bad behaviour. He waved the children over to the shop, where he gave them each an ice-cream to cool down.

'Are you okay?' Will asked Clementine. 'Joshua's always showing off and pushing people around.'

The girl nodded and wiped her eyes with the back of her hand.

'Don't worry about him,' Sophie said as the group sat on the bench, licking their ice-creams. Claws was lolling about on the footpath at their feet.

'He thinks he's the best at everything,' Teddy said. 'I wish he was allowed to audition for the show just so someone could have told him no.'

'That would have made him even madder,' Tilda agreed.

Clementine gasped and jumped to her feet. She had an idea and needed to tell Mr Loveberry about it straight away. There wasn't a moment to lose. 'I've got to go. Bye, everyone, and thank you for the ice-cream, Mr Mogg!'

Clementine looked left and right, then ran across the road and into the hall. She dodged past crewmen and contestants carrying their cakes until she found Mr Loveberry. He was wiping his fingers after a spectacularly messy tiramisu.

'Excuse me, Mr Loveberry,' the girl panted, 'could I tell you my idea for a –'

'Not now,' Florence Loveberry said, shooing the girl away with a flick of the wrist. She turned to her husband and held up two photographs. 'What do you think of this one, Nobby? I suspect *she* is in danger of being too sickly sweet, but her talent is undeniable. *He* is dull as dishwater, but we could find a way to spice things up. We have to think about the ratings, after all.'

Clementine could feel tears pricking the backs of her eyes. Her shin was throbbing in the spot where Joshua had kicked her and she suddenly wanted to go home. Mr Loveberry smiled at her and whispered that they would talk later, but it was no use. Clementine could feel a dark cloud settling over her.

What did lift her spirits somewhat was the sight of Mrs Mogg walking over with her cake. The woman had been in the shop all day, her till running hot as she sold snacks aplenty to the people queueing to audition. At one point she had had to rescue the cake she planned to present to the Loveberrys as her husband almost sold it right out from under her nose. They'd been so busy he'd forgotten that she hadn't been across to the hall yet.

'Well, I say,' Nobby Loveberry declared. He swallowed a bite of the Victoria sponge. 'What a highlight – and we've tasted some delicious cakes today.'

Mrs Loveberry raised her nose into the air and sniffed like a beagle on the hunt. 'What *is* that flavour?'

'It's a zesty lemon from the tree at the back of my shop,' Mrs Mogg said, smiling. She dusted her hands on her apron and sat down to do her screen test. Although the woman had confessed to being a bundle of nerves, she turned out to be a natural in front of the camera. Clementine, having forgotten the dark cloud, beamed with pride and gave the woman a double thumbs up.

Last but not least, Mrs Bottomley presented

her cake, and Nobby and Florence were once again in raptures over the peach creation.

'I, um, wanted to thank you both for giving me the opportunity to try,' the woman said, her hands clasped and her eyes rooted to the floor. 'Just the fact that you appreciate my baking has made me feel at least a little worthy.'

'How do you mean, Mrs Bottomley?' Nobby asked.

Ethel's eyes flitted to meet his and a sad smile crept onto her lips. 'Well, you see, my late mother-in-law was a talented baker. No matter how hard I tried, I never quite lived up to her standards. She took great pleasure in telling me I was a terrible cook – that I was terrible at everything, really.'

'Fantastic,' Florence Loveberry murmured, scribbling in her notebook.

Clementine felt a pang in her chest. She didn't think that sounded fantastic at all. It had never occurred to her that someone could make Mrs Bottomley feel that way.

Clementine thought of how her mother and Uncle Digby and Aunt Violet were always on hand with an encouraging word. She decided to write Mrs Bottomley a letter, but first she had the urge to run home and give her mother a great big hug.

A BUN IN THE OVEN

Clementine was hopscotching along the garden path when a pair of black polished shoes came into view. She stopped and looked up to find Dr Everingham standing before her. He was carrying his black bag and had just come down the back steps.

'Hello Clementine,' he said, smiling broadly. 'How were the auditions? I heard the queue at the village hall went for miles.'

'They weren't as exciting as I'd hoped,' the girl answered truthfully. 'And Joshua Tribble kicked me.'

The doctor bit back a smile. 'That doesn't sound good at all. Would you like me to take a look?'

'No, thank you. Mr Mogg gave me an ice-cream, so I'm beginning to feel better.' Clementine paused, a worry line appearing on her brow. 'Are you here because of Mummy? She's been feeling awful.'

'Poor thing has had a terrible time of it, but she's going to be fine. Turns out she has a bun in the oven. Terrific news, isn't it?' Dr Everingham rocked on his heels and grinned. 'Well, I best be off to my next appointment. I'll see you soon, Clemmie.' He waved goodbye and strode around the corner.

Clementine raced up the steps and in through the back door, hoping to see her mother and perhaps one or two of those famous Loveberry buns. But it was Uncle Digby who was busy at the stove with an apron tied around his waist. There were no buns in sight.

The man turned around. 'Hello Clemmie, you've had a long day.'

Clementine pulled out a chair and sat at the kitchen table. 'I'm 'sausted,' she said, cradling her chin in both hands.

'I bet you are. What have you done with the others?'

'Will stayed with Drew to help pack up and Granny's –'

'Right here,' the woman said, breezing into the room with a long-stemmed red rose in her hand.

'Who's been giving you flowers?' Uncle Digby asked, a curious expression on his face.

Violet tapped his nose with the flower and winked. 'Wouldn't you like to know.'

'Granny just picked it from the garden,' Clementine said, earning herself a glare from the old woman. She hopped down from her chair and went to give Lavender and Pharaoh a pat. 'Where's Mummy?' she asked.

Digby filled a tiny crystal-cut vase with an inch of water and passed it to Violet with a sweeping bow. 'She's upstairs, having a rest,' he answered. 'The doctor's been to see her this afternoon.'

'I saw Dr Everingham in the garden and he told me Mummy was here with a bun in the oven, but that wasn't true at all,' Clementine said, frowning. She still wasn't sure what to make of it. It wasn't like the doctor to get it so wrong.

Aunt Violet gasped and almost dropped the vase. She looked at Digby, who nodded. 'Well, what a day,' she said, smiling like she knew a delicious secret.

Clementine lifted Lavender into her arms and cuddled the little pig close. 'Let's go and say hello to Mummy,' she whispered, and padded up the back stairs.

Clementine knocked on her mother's bedroom door and poked her head around. She put Lavender down and tiptoed into the room, trying not to make a sound, but Lavender's trotters *tip-tapping* on the timber floor eventually gave them away.

Clarissa stirred and opened her eyes. 'Hello you two,' she said sleepily. 'How did it go today?'

'It was okay,' the child said, clambering onto the bed and snuggling in beside her mother.

Clarissa placed an arm around her. 'Just okay?'

'Joshua was there and he was really mean,' Clementine began and, before she knew it, the whole story came out in a rush of words and sniffles. 'I tried to tell Mr Loveberry my idea, but his horrible wife shooed me away.'

Clarissa touched the tip of her daughter's nose. 'Oh, darling, I'm sorry it wasn't as much fun as you'd hoped, and don't worry about Joshua. That boy is a menace to society, but he'll grow out of it before too much longer. And I think your idea is fabulous.'

'Are you feeling any better?' Clementine sniffled. 'Lavender wants to know too.' She had

picked up the little pig and put her on the bed with them.

'I'll be fine,' Clarissa promised.

There was a gentle knock and Aunt Violet pushed open the door. 'Hello dear,' she said, smiling widely. 'I thought you might like a cup of tea and something to nibble.'

'Thank you,' Clarissa said, pushing herself up against the pillows. 'After days of not being able to keep a single crumb down, I'm famished. I'm sorry to be so useless at the moment. I hope the Loveberrys are enjoying their stay.'

'Well, Mr Loveberry is perfectly charming. The same, however, cannot be said for that uppity wife of his,' Violet replied, her lips tightening at the mention of the woman. 'But she's nothing we can't handle. Isn't that right, Clemmie?'

'I suppose she's not the worst guest we've ever had,' Clementine replied with a little giggle.

'Now, come along. We should leave your mother to rest and concentrate on other things,' Aunt Violet said, raising an eyebrow at Clarissa. 'Clemmie, you can help me set the dining table.'

Clementine sighed and rolled off the edge of the bed. She didn't want to go, but waved goodbye and stepped out into the hall. While Aunt Violet and Lavender headed to the kitchen, Clementine decided to squeeze in a quick chat with her grandparents. She jumped down one step at a time until she reached the portraits along the staircase. Clementine often spoke to them, especially when something was troubling her. She began to tell them about her day and didn't hear the door to the Rose Room open or the footsteps in the hall.

Nobby Loveberry stopped when he reached the corner. By the tone of the girl's voice and the accompanying sniffles, he thought he ought not interrupt. It took him another moment to realise that the conversation was completely one-sided.

'I'm worried about Mummy,' Clementine confessed. 'She never gets sick and now she's in bed all the time and has a sieve for a brain. Not only that, I wasn't allowed to audition today and I really wanted to because then maybe it wouldn't seem so bad that it's all happening when we were supposed to be having our holidays together. Everyone is so busy and, even though they promise we can do some of the things we'd planned, I know we won't.'

Nobby Loveberry felt a tear spring to his eye. He brushed it away and continued listening.

'I tried to tell Mr Loveberry my idea about having a bake-off competition for kids. I had worked it all out too. We could sell the cakes afterwards and the money could go to charity, but Mrs Loveberry shooed me away before I could say anything,' Clementine said. 'Anyway, I'd better go. Aunt Violet – I mean, Granny – wants me to set the table. Thanks for listening. You always make me feel better, even though you never say anything back.'

Clementine stood up and straightened the bow in her hair.

Nobby took his cue, skipping down the stairs to meet her. 'Hello there, Clemmie,' he said brightly. 'You are just the person I was looking for. Perhaps you could help me with something?'

'Me?' Clementine said. 'I'll try.'

'You see, all those children who turned up at the audition today got me thinking about having a junior bake-off for charity. We could film it on the last day, just after announcing the winner of the competition, then sell the cakes to the families and friends who come along for the picnic. What do you think?' he asked.

Clementine's blue eyes widened. She looked at the portraits on the wall then back at Mr Loveberry. 'Are you a psycho?' she asked in a voice filled with awe. 'Because that's exactly what I was trying to tell you this afternoon.'

Nobby laughed, realising the girl had got herself muddled. 'I think you mean a psychic, Clemmie, and no, I'm not one of those. But perhaps the junior bake-off was written in the stars.'

Clementine liked the sound of that. She grinned, then remembered something. 'But what about Mrs Loveberry?' she asked.

'Oh, I wouldn't worry about her,' Nobby said with a wink. 'Leave it with me.'

Strawberry Kisses

The back garden was a hive of activity when Violet Appleby pulled up in the gravel driveway on Monday afternoon. There were trucks and workmen everywhere. Clementine, Will, Tilda and Teddy bounded out of the car and scampered off to investigate the fancy marquee that had sprung up in the middle of the back lawn. When they pressed their faces against the plastic windows, they were surprised to see six fully equipped kitchen stations in various stages of installation. After touring the rest of the set, the foursome barrelled into the kitchen, where Lavender and Pharaoh were both fast asleep in their basket.

'Hello you lot. How was school?' Clarissa asked. She hastily stuffed something inside the pages of an open recipe book and closed it.

'Everyone is so excited about the junior bake-off competition,' Clementine fizzed. 'Mr Smee announced it at assembly.'

'And Joshua got into trouble for calling out that he was going to be the winner,' Tilda added with a satisfied nod.

Clarissa laughed. 'Well, I'm glad it all worked out in the end. Now, who'd like some afternoon tea?'

There was a chorus of yeses from the children.

'You sit there, Clarissa,' Aunt Violet instructed as she placed a bag of groceries on the bench, and Digby set a box of fruit and vegetables beside it. 'Pertwhistle and

I can arrange something for the children to eat.'

Clarissa frowned. 'But I'm feeling much better.'

'Yes, but we don't want you overdoing it,' the woman said sternly.

Drew walked in from the hallway and gave his wife a peck on the cheek. 'I agree,' he said, stifling a yawn.

'Everyone needs to stop this at once. I'm perfectly fine,' Clarissa insisted, looking bemused. 'Now, I'm going to pick some flowers from the front garden and I won't hear another word about it.' She stood up and hurried out before anyone could object.

Clementine fetched some coloured paper and pens. She didn't understand why everyone was causing such a fuss when her mother had said she was feeling much better. Grown-ups were confusing at the best of times.

'Anyone fancy helping me move the woodpile?' Drew asked.

Will and Teddy were on it like a shot. They would have agreed to anything just to avoid doing their homework.

Clementine shook her head. 'Me and Tilda are going to make posters for the junior bake-off to put up around the school. Mrs Mogg said we can put one in her shop window too.'

'Oh, of course!' Drew said. 'Nobby told me about your brilliant idea. Well done, Clemmie. We're all very proud of you.' He gave her a wink and headed outside with the boys.

'Granny, can me and Tilda make a cake after we finish the posters?' Clementine asked, her legs swinging back and forth beneath the table. 'We need to practise for the bake-off.'

'Tilda and I,' Violet corrected from where she was unpacking the groceries. 'And, no, not today. Digby and I have to get on with the dinner. You can practise another afternoon when we aren't so busy.'

Clementine rolled her eyes at Tilda, who rolled hers too and then giggled into her hand. Digby poured the girls a glass of milk each and placed a plate of choc-chip cookies on the table before making a start on dinner. Aunt Violet washed three punnets of strawberries that were to be served with cream for dessert.

Clementine watched Uncle Digby and Aunt Violet for a moment with her head cocked to one side. There was something different about them, but she couldn't quite put her finger on it. She eventually gave up and went back to drawing a three-tiered cake, missing the moment the old man leant over to plant a kiss on the old woman's blushing cheek.

Practice Makes ... A Perfect Mess

The rest of the week flew by. Clementine returned from school each day to find everyone rushing about, preparing the house for *The Great Village Bake-Off.* Not only was the show to be filmed at Penberthy House, but all the contestants had to reside there for the duration of the competition as a safeguard against cheating. It was going to be a full house as of Tuesday, when they were all due to arrive. The competition would begin the following day and continue until the grand finale picnic on Sunday. Everyone was so busy that Clementine hadn't been able to practise her baking at all. Joshua Tribble, on the other hand, had brought in a different cake to school each day. Clementine didn't like to admit it, but they were delicious.

On Saturday morning, school holidays had officially begun and Clementine was keen to start baking. She asked Aunt Violet to help her, but the woman had been called upon to replace one of the models in a seniors fashion parade who'd had an unfortunate accident. Aunt Violet said she couldn't understand why Elaine hadn't asked her in the first place. Dolores Whitby couldn't walk in a straight line and it was a miracle she hadn't landed in someone's lap before now, which is precisely what had happened.

Undeterred, Clementine asked Uncle Digby, but it turned out he was busy as well, having to do all the shopping for the week. Drew and Will were on their way to the city to pick up some equipment for the production.

They invited Clementine to join them, but she didn't want to spend the first day of her holiday on a long car ride. Plus, if she didn't start practising, she wouldn't stand a chance in the competition.

Clementine looked at the kitchen clock. It was almost half past ten and, besides the odd creak and groan, the house was quiet as a church mouse. She walked over to the dresser and picked up her mother's special recipe book. It had lots of handwritten pages and bits and pieces of magazines cut out and stuffed inside. Some of the dishes dated back nearly one hundred years and had come from Clementine's great-grandmother, though her mother and Uncle Digby had added lots of new ones too.

Clementine knew she wasn't supposed to cook on her own, so she decided to pick what cake she'd like to bake first. She placed the recipe book on the kitchen table and hopped up on the chair, carefully opening the first page.

'What should we make, Lavender?' she asked the little pig, who was snuffling about under her chair. Clementine turned the page and gasped. 'I know! Grandma Phil's light, fluffy chocolate cake.'

Lavender grunted her approval while Pharaoh padded into the room from the pantry, licking his lips. Clementine hoped he hadn't got into anything he shouldn't have.

'Mummy!' Clementine called up the back stairs.

When there was no reply, the girl bounded up to the top floor and raced along the hall. She knocked on her mother's bedroom door and turned the handle, surprised to find Clarissa sound asleep. Her mother was taking more naps than Claws these days – she'd even fallen asleep at the breakfast table. Clementine sighed, then gently closed the door and headed back to the kitchen.

'Never mind,' Clementine said to Lavender and Pharaoh. 'We can make Mummy a surprise.'

When neither of them disagreed, she fetched the stool and began gathering the ingredients from the baking shelf in the pantry. Her mother was a stickler for labels and Clementine's reading was excellent these days, so it didn't take her long to gather everything she needed. Clementine put on her apron and pulled the big mixing bowl from the cupboard, then set to work.

Measuring the flour, sugar and cocoa into the bowl was easy enough. Clementine may have spilt a bit here and there, but she would wipe it up later. Adding the eggs was a tad trickier. Two of them landed with a *splat* on the floor before she managed to get the rest into the bowl. Luckily, Lavender was on hand to lap up the mess.

'Thank you,' Clementine said, admiring the way the tiny pig's trotters were making patterns in the flour.

Next up was the milk. Clementine held the measuring jug with both hands and managed to only splash a little of it. She hadn't yet

noticed the milk carton had been left on its side and was now feeding a steady waterfall down the kitchen cabinets. Clementine hopped off the stool and, standing on tippy-toes, pushed the bowl along the bench and under the mixer. She hit the switch and watched as the beaters began to spin.

She hoped her mother would be up soon. Clementine wasn't supposed to touch the oven on her own and it made her feel jittery in the tummy just thinking about it. Sometimes, when no one else was around, the oven made mean faces at her. Clementine snuck a look at it when the front doorbell rang.

'This isn't a good time for visitors,' Clementine grumbled.

She hopped down from the stool then realised that she had left the beaters turning. She scurried back up and lifted them from the bowl, forgetting to turn off the machine first. Big brown splodges of cake mix flew through the air, spraying everything within sight. Clementine quickly flicked the switch.

She grabbed a tea towel and wiped her hands, but the rest would have to wait as the doorbell would not stop ringing.

'I'm coming!' Clementine called, charging through the swinging door and down the hallway to the entrance foyer. She didn't want her mother to wake up before she had time to clean the mess. Lavender ran at the girl's heels, leaving a trail of cake batter mixed with flour and raw egg in her wake. Clementine opened the door and came face to face with Mrs Bottomley.

'Hello Clementine, is Violet about?' Ethel asked, looking at the girl curiously. 'And what's happened to you and the pig?'

Clementine glanced down at her apron. It looked like a Kindergarten spatter painting. Suddenly, a crash sounded from the kitchen.

'What on earth was that?' Mrs Bottomley said.

Clementine gasped and tore back down the hall with Mrs Bottomley hot on her heels. She burst through the kitchen door to find Pharaoh sitting on the bench with a chocolate moustache on his guilty lips and the mixing bowl smashed all over the floor. 'Naughty Pharaoh,' she scolded. 'You don't even like cake and you're not allowed to have chocolate.'

The sphynx cat jumped down to the floor and scurried up the back stairs and out of sight.

Mrs Bottomley's eyes were the size of dinner plates as she took in the mess. 'Good heavens, it looks like a chocolate factory exploded in here.'

Clementine bit her lip, bracing herself for a scolding. 'I was making a surprise for Mummy,' she explained. 'All I wanted was to practise for the junior bake-off, but everyone was too busy to help me. Now all I've made is a disaster.'

'Dear me, never mind,' the woman said. She used her finger to wipe a glob of cake mixture from a cupboard door and popped it into her mouth. 'Ooh, that's ghastly!' she exclaimed, pulling a face. Mrs Bottomley examined the ingredients on the bench and realised the child's mistake. 'I hate to break it to you, dear, but no one was going to enjoy that cake of yours. What do you think this is?' she asked, holding up a little container.

'Sugar?' Clementine said, though she was no longer so sure.

Mrs Bottomley shook her head. 'Salt.'

'Oh.' Clementine bit her lip and blushed.

'Right, I suspect there's no time to waste.' Mrs Bottomley grabbed a cloth from the sink, then proceeded to attack every surface. She even scaled a ladder to get to the higher places. Clementine gave Lavender a thorough wiping down, then the two of them helped to clean the floor. The kitchen was back to normal in no time flat. 'Now, seeing as your grandmother has abandoned our game of bridge, how about I help you bake that cake?' Mrs Bottomley said. 'You were only trying to do a good deed and I'd hate for you to lose your love of baking for fear of getting things wrong, or someone telling you that you're hopeless.'

Clementine could hardly believe her ears. 'Thank you, Mrs Bottomley,' she said, meaning it.

'Well, don't just stand there, Clementine. If we're to surprise your mother, we'd best get on with it. And perhaps we can keep what happened earlier between us. There's no point upsetting everyone unnecessarily.'

The girl nodded and grinned. 'You know, Mrs Bottomley, you're not really as mean as everyone says.'

Ethel rolled her eyes and turned to switch on the oven. 'Honesty is certainly a virtue, but by golly, Clementine, you're becoming more like your grandmother by the day.'

SUGAR AND SPICE

Clementine's chocolate cake was a big hit with the family, including Clarissa, who appeared to have regained her appetite and then some. Thankfully, nobody thought to ask who had helped her with it. Clementine baked again on Sunday with Uncle Digby acting as her assistant. This time she whipped up a batch of butterfly cakes with cream frosting, and on Monday she made shortbread biscuits and a marble cake too. Clementine shared her treats with the film and production crew, who gobbled everything down with gusto. The girl even earned herself high praise from Mr Loveberry, who said her chocolate icing was perfect.

On Tuesday afternoon, the contestants were due to begin arriving from two o'clock. Drew and the crew were filming them from the moment the car turned into the driveway. Each was scheduled fifteen minutes apart as Basil wanted to capture the looks of surprise and delight on their faces when they were greeted by Nobby and Florence. The camera crews were set up out the front of the house, in the foyer and the sitting room.

Clementine couldn't wait to meet everyone. Although she and Will had been instructed to keep out of the way and watch the proceedings from their parents' bedroom window on the third floor, Clementine planned to introduce herself later.

'Don't you two look lovely,' Clarissa said.

Clementine had chosen to wear her favourite red dress, pink cardigan, white tights and red patent Mary Jane shoes. Will was in his good trousers and a long-sleeved shirt with the vest he wore to his father and Clarissa's wedding on top. The boy caught his stepsister's eye and the pair of them giggled. Not wanting to miss any of the action, they hurried upstairs and took a detour via Aunt Violet's room.

'Quick,' Clementine whispered. She looped several strands of pearls around her neck and clipped on a pair of Aunt Violet's pearl earrings. Will combed his hair flat and doused it with hairspray. He laughed as he watched Clementine apply a lathering of red lipstick.

The children then raced across to their parents' bedroom and positioned themselves at the window overlooking the entrance.

'Hello, my name is Florence Loveberry and this is my husband, Nobby. Welcome to *The Great Village Bake-Off*,' Clementine began in her poshest voice. 'Now, let's see who our first contestant is. Oh no, I forgot something!'

'What is it?' Will asked, but Clementine ran out of the room and returned, clutching a notebook and a pen.

The children were on the edge of their seats, waiting for the first guest to hop out of the car and were stunned to see Mr Moreno. Clementine squealed with delight when Mrs Mogg arrived next. She and Will agreed that they both thought the woman would win. The third contestant was the lovely Tiggy Edwards, and her dress this afternoon was even more beautiful than the one she'd worn to the audition. Then there was the youngest contestant to appear on the show – a boy of sixteen who was still in high school. His name was Zander Crowe, and Will reminded Clementine that his audition cake looked just like a Rubik's cube. There was a man called Axel Grimley who told really bad dad jokes but had presented a cake that looked like a speedboat. The children had a wonderful time commentating each arrival and managed to play several vigorous games of Go Fish between contestants.

Will had just thrown down two aces when the door opened and Aunt Violet walked in. 'What are you two up to?' she said, looking them up and down. 'Good heavens, are you pretending to be the Loveberrys? And are those my pearls, young lady?'

The children glanced at each other in alarm, hoping they weren't about to get told off.

'Golly, you look marvellous,' Violet said, chuckling. 'Although, Clementine, that's not even half as many pearls as Mrs Loveberry wears. That woman is a walking crime against fashion.'

Clementine and Will both breathed a sigh of relief.

'Well, there's a turn-up for the books,' the old woman said, peering over them.

The children looked out the window to see that the last contestant was none other than Mrs Bottomley. Clementine grinned, but before they could all celebrate, a bloodcurdling scream rocketed through the ancient house.

'HELP! Get it away from me!' a voice shrieked, followed by the sound of a door slamming.

'Who was that?' Will asked, running out into the hall.

The trio flew downstairs and found Zander Crowe cowering outside the Sage Room.

'Help,' he whimpered, his face crumpling. 'There's a giant rat in there and I think it was eating a piglet.'

'What's going on?' Drew asked, speeding up the staircase with Basil right behind him. The Loveberrys and Clarissa brought up the rear.

Clementine had a feeling she knew exactly what had happened. When Aunt Violet had first arrived at Penberthy House, Clementine had thought Pharaoh looked like a rodent or perhaps an alien. The girl placed her hand on the doorhandle and was about to enter the room when the young man blocked her path.

'What if it tries to eat you as well?' he said desperately.

By now, Zander's scream had drawn a crowd. All the other contestants had come to see what the commotion was about. Miss Edwards and Mrs Mogg began to fuss over the lad and Uncle Digby left to make him a cup of tea. Amid the chaos, Clementine ducked under the man's arms and opened the door. As she suspected, Lavender and Pharaoh were there to greet her. The cat was licking the inside of the tiny pig's left ear, where, Clementine realised, she must have missed some of the chocolate batter from the other day. She separated the two and passed Pharaoh to Will. Clementine picked up Lavender and nuzzled her against her cheek. The children emerged from the bedroom, and Zander, taking one look at Pharaoh, fainted to the floor.

'I hope someone got that on film,' Florence said, sniggering while the others attended to the lad. She ticked something in her notebook before snapping it shut and looking at Clementine. 'What on earth are you wearing?'

Clementine swallowed hard when she realised that she was still in her Mrs Loveberry dress-ups. 'I was, um, pretending to be –'

'Aunt Violet,' Will said quickly. 'Clemmie dressed up as Aunt Violet and I'm Uncle Digby. We were doing a play.'

'Good heavens – I don't know what you were thinking with that outfit, young lady,' Mrs Loveberry scoffed. 'It's absolutely ghastly.'

'I couldn't agree more,' Aunt Violet said, giving Clementine and Will a sly wink.

Zander began to rouse. He sat up groggily and the first thing he clapped eyes on was Pharaoh cradled in Will's arms. 'Ohhh,' he groaned again before his head hit the floor.

SWEET AS PIE

On Tuesday evening, with Lavender and Pharaoh banished to the Hobbs' house for the rest of the week, Will had opted for a sleepover too, citing that he and the twins wanted to build bike jumps in the woods. He had left out the part about not wanting to run into Mrs Bottomley or Mrs Loveberry roaming the halls of Penberthy House. Thankfully, after the initial hiccup, the contestants were all getting along like a house on fire. Aunt Violet had reported what a cheerful group they were when she served them canapés and drinks in the sitting room before dinner. Unfortunately, Clarissa had again taken to her bed, the smell of roasting meat turning her a ghastly shade of green.

Clementine was sitting at the kitchen table, wondering if she should have gone with Will, while Uncle Digby wrestled a giant leg of lamb out of the oven. Aunt Violet was busy spooning the roast vegetables into silver serving dishes.

'Can I help carry something?' Clementine asked. She was dying to meet the contestants properly and see what was going on in the dining room.

'We're fine, thank you, Clemmie,' Uncle Digby said. 'Why don't you have a look at some recipes and decide what you'd like to bake tomorrow?'

Clementine supposed she could do that. She chose a book that she'd never looked at before. It had all sorts of fancy cakes inside with very long lists of ingredients and lots and lots of writing. Once she had chosen a polka-dot strawberry cake, Clementine decided to speak to her grandparents. She had just settled on the step with the best view of the portraits along the wall when she heard Mrs Loveberry approach, talking loudly on her phone.

'Urgh, they're all so jolly nice to each other! And that Tiggy Edwards has everyone eating out of the palm of her hand with that sweet as pie act she's got going on. It's going to make for dreadful television,' the woman complained. 'Anyway, Susan, I have to go. I've had a thought. Wish us luck, and next time I'd appreciate it if your children didn't come down with chicken pox while we're in the middle of a show. It's very inconvenient.'

Clementine leaned over the banister to see Mrs Loveberry trotting back to join the others. Seconds later, it sounded as if someone had thrown a hand grenade into the dining room. Clementine hurried downstairs and poked her head around the door.

'Youth does not always trump experience, young man,' Mr Moreno said loudly. 'We're not losers because we're old. Just you wait and see.' There was a thump on the table.

'Well, I don't think old age means you know it all either,' Zander crowed. 'Young people are capable of many things.'

'We were young once too,' Axel Grimley said.

'None of us is especially old now,' Tiggy Edwards added, smoothing her skirt. She threw a nervous glance the Loveberrys' way.

Margaret Mogg frowned. 'I am, dear, and Ethel's not exactly a spring chicken.'

'I never said you were old,' Zander said crossly.

Nobby Loveberry bit his lip. He'd been enjoying himself far more when everyone was getting along. Clementine noticed the smug look on Mrs Loveberry's face.

Aunt Violet and Uncle Digby entered the hall with the dessert trays.

'What are you up to, Clemmie?' Uncle Digby asked. His eyebrows jumped up as he registered the raised voices coming from the room. There was quite the argument in full flight. 'Heavens, who knew that home bakers were such a rowdy bunch.'

Clementine was desperate to bake the polka-dot strawberry cake, but Uncle Digby said he had lots of jobs to do that morning and so did her mother and Aunt Violet. After an hour or so of being bored, Clementine picked up her skipping rope and headed downstairs. It was too beautiful a day to be cooped up inside, plus she wanted to see how many times she could skip around the circular drive without stopping. After two full rounds, Clementine had run out of puff and took herself off to the side of the house in the shade. She was about to sit on the steps when she spotted Miss Edwards standing beneath the weeping willow near the garage, almost hidden from view. The woman pulled something from her pocket and studied it.

'Hello,' Clementine said, causing Miss Edwards to jump. 'Are you all right?'

The woman smiled tightly and gripped whatever she was holding firmly in her hand. 'Yes, of course. Why wouldn't I be? Sorry, I have to get back.' Miss Edwards hurried away, around the corner of the house to the back garden.

Clementine decided to follow her. They must have taken a break in filming and she was keen to sneak a peek at the contestants' creations. She turned the corner and was surprised to find that the cameras were still rolling. Miss Edwards rushed back to her station at the rear of the tent.

The Loveberrys were standing opposite Mr Grimley, and the three of them seemed to be having a terrific time. On the other side of the marquee, however, it was a different matter. Mrs Bottomley looked as if she'd swallowed a bucket of lemons. Florence and

Nobby Loveberry approached her bench, shaking their heads. It was clear that whatever Mrs Bottomley had baked had not gone well.

Once the cameras stopped rolling, Mrs Mogg hurried over to console the woman, who was dabbing at her eyes with a scrunched-up tissue. Clementine set her skipping rope down near the entrance and made her way over to see what had happened. 'What's the matter, Mrs Bottomley?' the child asked. She caught sight of the cake on the stand. On the outside it looked perfect, but where the Loveberrys had cut into it, a chocolate-cherry ooze was spreading everywhere. 'Is it meant to do that?' she asked.

'No, and I've never had a black forest cake fail me,' Ethel wept. 'I followed that recipe to the letter of the law. Unless there's something wrong with that oven or someone substituted one of the ingredients, I don't know what happened.'

'Who would do that? We were all here and provided with the exact same things,' Mrs Mogg said. She patted Ethel's hand.

'We all have our bad days, dear, but you have many chances yet to prove yourself in the competition. Now, chin up. It's nothing a cup of tea can't fix.'

Clementine looked around at what everyone else had created. Mr Moreno's black forest cake was standing tall, but instead of being decorated with cherries, he'd used strawberries, which Clementine had a feeling wasn't right. Miss Edwards' cake was lovely, as was Mrs Mogg's. Axel Grimley's was leaning a little to one side, but Zander Crowe's looked like something from a magazine. It was nothing short of magnificent.

It was fair to say that the atmosphere inside the marquee was rather subdued. Despite Nobby Loveberry wearing his trademark grin, the man couldn't help thinking it was strange that Ethel's cake had been such a disaster. He'd watched her while she was making it and thought she was very precise. Perhaps there was a problem with her oven. Nobby made a note to ask one of the tradesmen to look into it right away.

TROUBLE BREWING

'Please can we make the strawberry polka-dot cake this afternoon, Uncle Digby?' Clementine asked.

'Sounds delicious, Clemmie, but goodness me, I'll be glad when the bake-off is done and dusted.' Digby Pertwhistle patted his stomach. 'My pants are getting tighter by the day. And that does look a little complicated.'

Clementine grinned. 'It's meant to be hard, silly. How am I supposed to get better if I don't challenge myself? Plus you're the skinniest person I know except for Aunt Violet – I mean Granny.'

'Your grandmother has a lovely figure,' Uncle Digby said with a nod.

'Do I now?' The old woman arched her left eyebrow as she walked down the back stairs into the kitchen.

Digby Pertwhistle's cheeks flushed pink, although Clementine could have sworn she saw him wink at the woman. Something strange was going on with those two, that was for sure. Aunt Violet would normally have ripped Uncle Digby's head off for saying something like that, but then again, he had paid her a compliment. Maybe that was the difference, Clementine surmised.

She set about fetching the ingredients from the pantry and laid out everything across the bench. Clementine then pulled the mixing bowl from the cupboard beneath the counter. After lining it all up, she realised there was one thing she didn't have and, without it, the cake wouldn't work at all. She was missing red and pink food colouring.

'You could pop downstairs to see if they have any spare,' Digby suggested. 'There's just about every ingredient known to man in the supplies store.'

'They're due to start filming again in fifteen minutes,' Aunt Violet said as she filled the kettle, 'so you'd better hurry.'

'Good idea,' Clementine said, and hopped off her little stool.

For the duration of the bake-off competition, the cellar had been transformed into something resembling a baker's wonderland. There were sacks of flour and sugar of every description, molasses, baking powder, chocolate, spices, fresh and dried fruit, nuts, dozens upon dozens of eggs, extra cake tins and pans, spare spatulas and mixing bowls and lots of other things Clementine had never seen before.

She raced out the back, where several crew members were busy stocking the fridges and cupboards of each kitchen in the marquee. The contestants were milling about in their aprons, nervously awaiting their next instructions, and Mrs Loveberry was scribbling in her notebook as usual. Clementine checked with Mr Loveberry that it was all right for her to borrow some food colouring, then ran down to the cellar and hunted about. It didn't take her too long to locate a bottle of red food colouring and another of pink, but just as she was about to leave, she heard footsteps on the stairs and a familiar voice. It was Mrs Mogg and she sounded as if she was on the phone.

'Yes, Clyde, I know how important this is for us,' the woman said in hushed tones. 'I'm doing everything I can.'

Clementine ducked down behind a huge tin of olive oil.

'I have to go. We're about to start filming and please don't call me again – I shouldn't even be talking to you now,' Margaret said. She popped her phone back into her apron pocket and hurried upstairs.

Clementine's tummy twisted. She knew Mrs Mogg was breaking the rules by talking on her phone because she'd heard Uncle Digby say that contestants weren't supposed to be communicating with their family and friends until Sunday. It must have been an emergency because Margaret Mogg was just about the most honest person Clementine knew. She wouldn't cheat . . . That wouldn't make any sense at all.

HALF-BAKED

Clementine's strawberry polka-dot cake was a complete flop. She hadn't been able to get the imprints of the strawberries right on the outside, so they just looked like brown blobs and the apricot jam for the top had formed sugar crystals. Not one to be deterred, Clementine tried her hand at a coconut and passionfruit mousse the next day, but it simply refused to set. All of the difficult recipes she attempted ended in disaster, and she still had no idea what she was going to make for the junior bake-off. In a strange twist of fate, it seemed that the contestants were facing similar challenges, with everyone experiencing at least two failures.

'I think there's a saboteur among us,' Mr Moreno said while the group was having morning tea in the sitting room.

Mrs Loveberry turned to the man. 'What nonsense! Who has the time or the inclination?'

Aunt Violet was pouring the tea while Clementine offered everyone peppermint slices that her mother had helped her make after the awful mousse. Florence Loveberry batted her hand, but Mr Loveberry reached out eagerly and at first bite declared it the most delicious thing he'd tasted all day. The claim garnered glares from some of the contestants.

Margaret Mogg sighed and shook her head. 'I have no idea how my passionfruit sponge collapsed,' she fretted. 'I've made that cake countless times over three decades and it's been perfect until this morning.'

Axel Grimley nodded. 'The mystery of my butter cake with the consistency of rubber will haunt me forever.'

The contestants eyed each other warily.

'Well, I saw Ethel with her head in Zander's fridge,' Mr Moreno said, turning to the woman. 'I bet you took his buttermilk and replaced it with something else, didn't you?'

Mrs Bottomley's face turned bright red. She leapt to her feet and towered over the man. 'I did no such thing! *I* suspect it is *you* who has been tampering with our ingredients. You're always lurking about in the shadows and disappearing right when we're supposed to begin filming. Where do you go?' she yelled, her eyes wild with rage. 'Unless you've got a toilet issue?'

The man's jaw gaped open.

'Well, I think it's you!' Mr Grimley pointed at Tiggy Edwards, who almost dropped her teacup in fright.

'W-Why?' the woman stuttered, resembling a deer in headlights. 'W-What did I ever do to you?'

'Nobody could be so sweet and so . . . so *floral*,' the man accused. 'Plus I've seen you exit the marquee a few times during filming. Where do you go?'

Clementine bit her lip. She wished Mr Smee was here. The grown-ups were behaving worse than her Year One class on a bad day and he could always wrangle them back into shape. Come to think of it, she had seen all of the contestants behave in ways that weren't entirely in keeping with the rules. Except for Mrs Bottomley, that is.

'My, my, I must say we have never had a bake-off competition so hotly contested.' Mr Loveberry chuckled. 'It will be fabulous for ratings and leaves things wide open for tomorrow's finale.'

Mrs Loveberry grinned from ear to ear. It was true. There were only three points separating the entire group, so who would emerge as the ultimate winner was anyone's guess.

With huffs and puffs and the slamming of doors, the contestants retired to their rooms. They were due to resume filming in half an hour, but it seemed they were all keen to take some time out. Clementine helped Aunt Violet and Uncle Digby clear the dishes, then sat at the kitchen table, wondering what Lavender was up to. Will returned home a short while later and was thumbing through a magazine about mountain bikes.

'Do you really think someone could be sabotating the contestants?' Clementine asked.

Clarissa emerged from the pantry, eating sardines straight from the tin. 'I think you mean sabotaging, Clemmie,' she said with a giggle.

'If my many years on this earth have taught me one lesson, it's that anything is possible,' Aunt Violet said, pulling on a pair of rubber gloves. 'But, my goodness, they're a passionate bunch, aren't they?'

'Maybe you should become a detective, Clemmie,' Uncle Digby suggested.

'I'll help,' Will volunteered. He loved playing Cluedo and working out mysteries and now they had a real-life one to solve.

Clementine nodded and pushed back her chair. 'Come on,' she said, heading for the back stairs. 'We can use the whiteboard in my room to write down all the evidence.'

VOILÀ!

Clementine began to jot down all the strange happenings she'd seen and heard since the competition had started. She wrote down the contestants' names and used lots of lines and squiggles the way Mr Smee did when he created mind maps on the board at school.

'They aren't meant to talk on their phones, but I've seen Mrs Mogg and Mr Grimley on theirs,' Clementine said. 'And when you were away, Mr Moreno had a big argument with Zander and Mr Grimley and even Miss Edwards joined in too. I saw Mr Grimley in the library and he was scribbling something down, which he hid as soon as he noticed me.'

Will agreed there were a lot of weird coincidences, but none of them proved any of the contestants' guilt. 'Maybe we need to go and watch them and make notes,' he suggested. 'We can be proper detectives.'

'Like Mrs Loveberry,' Clementine said. 'She writes in that notebook of hers all the time. It's never out of her hand. I think it must be more precious than her pearls.'

Will was standing at the window that overlooked the back garden. 'We could watch them from here,' he said. He wasn't keen to get too close to Mrs Bottomley or Mrs Loveberry.

Clementine shook her head. 'It's better from the garden.' She snatched up a pencil and the notebook from her desk and charged into the hallway with her stepbrother behind her.

The children ran downstairs and out through the patio doors, then hid behind the oak tree, where they had a good view. Mr and Mrs Loveberry were moving through the marquee talking to each contestant, who all seemed to be busy either sifting flour or cracking eggs or whisking their mixtures.

Clementine opened her notebook and wrote a heading at the top of the page. Will leaned over and pointed out that the word 'clues' was spelt with a 'u' and an 'e' instead of a double 'o'. Clementine crossed out the heading and rewrote it correctly.

After five minutes, Will began drawing in the dirt with a stick and Clementine was watching a trail of ants marching up the tree. Mrs Loveberry headed inside but Mr Loveberry stayed in the tent, although he was out of shot of the cameras.

Clementine sighed. 'It's a bit boring being a detective.'

'We need some binoculars so we can see things up close,' Will said.

Clementine nodded. 'That's a great idea! There are some on Grandpa's desk in the library.' She shot off through the patio doors and along the hallway. Coming in from the bright sunshine, the children didn't notice Mrs Loveberry striding towards them. Clementine charged straight into her, sending the glass of iced water in the woman's hand skywards. Fortunately, Will's reflexes were excellent and he dived to catch the tumbler before it hit the ground. But the damage was already done.

'Aarghh!' Florence Loveberry shrieked as an ice cube plunged down the front of her blouse. 'You stupid children!'

Clementine gasped. 'Sorry, Mrs Loveberry. I'll get a towel.'

'Don't bother!' Florence huffed. She dropped her notebook and fountain pen on the hall table and fled into the downstairs powder room.

Clementine eyed the notebook, which hadn't escaped unscathed. 'We should try to dry it, or else we'll be in bigger trouble when Mrs Loveberry comes back,' she said.

Clementine mopped at the cover with a tissue, then opened the notebook to dab at the damp pages. She gasped as she took in the words on the page. 'Will,' Clementine whispered, 'look at this.'

The boy leaned over to take a look, his eyes widening in surprise.

The sound of footsteps on the timber floor prompted Clementine to glance up just in time. She closed the notebook as Florence Loveberry barrelled towards them, muttering about her hair. 'We'd better not run behind because of your carelessness,' the woman barked, snatching up her notebook and pen. 'And you can bring me another glass of iced water!'

'Should we tell Dad?' Will whispered as the woman disappeared outside.

Clementine thought for a moment and, suddenly, she knew exactly what they needed to do.

'I can't believe my cake was so bad,' Zander said, shaking his head. 'I did everything according to the recipe, but it tastes like dirt.'

Clementine and Will looked at each other. 'We know why,' Will said firmly.

The cast and crew turned to face the children, who were standing in the entrance of the marquee.

Drew sighed. 'Kids, please go back inside. We've only got a few more minutes of filming left and then you can come and chat to everyone.'

'But someone's cheating and that's why the cakes are all flopping,' Clementine said.

The contestants' brows furrowed like a farmer's field. They all shot suspicious glares at one another.

'I knew it!' Zander said, folding his arms across his chest. 'It's Mr Moreno.'

'Don't look at me,' the man retorted.

'No, it's Mrs Bottomley,' Miss Edwards squeaked. 'Never trust a woman who only wears one colour.'

Ethel Bottomley's brown hair stood on end. 'How dare you!'

The accusations were flying thick and fast until Clementine clapped her hands to get everyone's attention. 'I'm sorry to tell you this, Mr Loveberry, but Mrs Loveberry has been sabotating everyone,' she said in her most serious voice.

Will leaned over and whispered in his stepsister's ear.

'I mean sabotaging,' Clementine said with a firm nod.

Florence Loveberry's jaw almost hit the ground. 'What's the meaning of this outrage!'

Nobby Loveberry looked just as perplexed as the rest of the contestants. 'Florence, what are the children talking about?' he asked.

Florence Loveberry and her pearls bristled. 'How on earth would I know?' the woman spat. 'They're clearly wildly imaginative creatures or downright *liars*. Why would I sabotage my own show?'

'To make it more fun for the viewers,'

Clementine said. 'I heard you telling your daughter they were all so boring that no one would want to watch the show. So you swapped ingredients and took the seals off the ovens and made the timers wrong.'

'All the plans are in this notebook,' exclaimed Will as he snatched it out of Mrs Loveberry's hands and held it up. 'Mrs Loveberry kept track to make sure that the competition would be really close.'

Nobby looked at his wife as if for the first time – the disappointment in his eyes clear. 'Is this true?'

Florence Loveberry pursed her lips. 'Oh, all right. I admit it. I did it for us, Nobby,' she said, holding her head up high. 'It's just that this lot are so nice to each other and who's going to want to watch a show like that? I just spiced things up a bit, that's all. You do want our show to be a success, don't you?'

'Yes, of course I do, but not like this,' he replied, shaking his head. For the first time since Clementine had met him,

Nobby Loveberry didn't appear to be smiling. He turned to the contestants. 'I am so sorry for how badly we have treated you. If you'll accept our apologies, I will personally see to it that Florence will have nothing to do with the rest of the show. From now on, it will be a fair playing field.'

'But I *have* to be in the finale!' Florence wailed. '*I'm* the star!'

The contestants all looked as if they'd been stung by something very nasty. Basil and Drew shared a quizzical look.

Nobby shook his head. 'All right, Florence, you can still be in the finale, but I'll be watching you like a hawk.' He turned to Clementine and Will. 'Thank you, children. Without your detective skills, we'd have been none the wiser.'

Clementine grinned and Will beamed. 'Oh!' Clementine gasped. 'The junior bake-off is tomorrow and I still haven't decided what to make. Come on, Will, maybe you can help me decide.'

SWEET NOTHINGS

Clementine's eyes fluttered open. She'd had the most wonderful dream, in which she'd baked a cake that her mother always cooked for birthdays and family celebrations. It was simple and delicious and tasted just like love. And that, Clementine decided, was exactly what she was going to make for the junior bake-off.

She pushed back the covers and quickly got dressed, then bounced down to the kitchen. She was surprised to see her mother standing by the stove. Clarissa had on her apron and had already made a start on a batch of pancakes.

'Mummy!' the child squealed, rushing in for a hug.

Clarissa turned and met her with open arms. 'Hello darling.'

'Are you finally better?' Clementine asked, noticing the colour was back in her mother's cheeks. In fact, the woman was positively glowing.

'I feel wonderful, actually. Much, much better,' Clarissa said with a smile.

Digby bustled out of the pantry. He also had on an apron and looked ready for business.

Clementine fetched her mother's ancient recipe book from the shelf. She pulled it down and flicked through the pages then held up a strange-looking photograph. She studied it carefully, but it just looked like a blob. 'What's this?' Clementine asked, holding it out for her mother to see.

'Oh heavens.' Clarissa flew over and scooped it from the girl's hand. 'I couldn't for the life of me remember where I'd put that.'

'What is it a photo of?' Clementine asked. 'It's very blurry.'

'A surprise for later,' her mother replied with a wink.

'I hope it's a good surprise because I don't want any more bad ones after yesterday,' Clementine said, turning her attention back to the book.

Clarissa and Digby grinned knowingly.

'You can say that again,' Drew quipped as he walked into the room. 'Well done, Clemmie. You and Will should think about starting a detective agency.'

Clementine looked at her stepfather. 'I'm not sure about that. Detective work is a bit boring and I'm sorry I caused lots of trouble.'

The man frowned. 'Sweetheart, you made everything right. I wouldn't want to be involved in a show that was dishonest. At least all the contestants have had the same number of flops, so it wasn't too unfair.' He kissed the top of the child's golden head, then grabbed a pancake from the pile. 'I have to get going – lots to do this morning,' he said, and gave his wife a peck on the cheek. 'Good luck with your cake, Clemmie. I'm sure it will be wonderful.'

The happy threesome set to work. Clementine made the cake all by herself, only requiring help with the oven. Everything went according to plan and this time there was not one spill on the kitchen floor.

Aunt Violet glided into the room in a smart pair of cream trousers and a lovely red silk blouse. 'If that tastes anywhere near as good as it smells, Clemmie, you should win the junior bake-off hands down,' she declared cheerfully.

'I hope so,' Clementine replied with a grin. She watched the cake closely, hoping it wouldn't collapse in the middle. 'But Joshua Tribble brought some really delicious cakes to school last week, so he could win too.'

'Well, it will be interesting to see who comes up trumps in the grown-up's competition. It was lucky you outed Mrs Loveberry so they can now have a fair contest,' Aunt Violet said. She hurried over to help Digby plate up the breakfasts. 'Here, darling, I'll do that.'

Clementine gasped. 'Granny, you just called Uncle Digby "darling".'

'Oh, did I?' The old woman smiled. 'How silly of me. I meant to say "dragon face", of course.'

Clementine laughed. 'You two are funny.'

'Indeed we are,' Uncle Digby said, and planted a kiss right on Aunt Violet's lips.

Clarissa smiled at the pair. Will, who had just arrived on the scene, had half a mind to turn around and scurry back up the stairs. For a moment he wondered if he was in the right house.

'Granny, is Uncle Digby your boyfriend?' Clementine asked.

'Something like that,' the woman replied.

Clementine giggled. She thought it was nothing short of a miracle that two people who had once detested each other were now in love. The girl's eyes widened as another thought occurred to her. It was too horrible to say aloud. If Aunt Violet and Uncle Digby could love each other, maybe she and Joshua Tribble might love each other too one day. Clementine squeezed her eyes shut and pushed that awful thought right out of her head.

THE ICING ON THE CAKE

Everyone was set to arrive for the grand finale of *The Great Village Bake-Off* at one o'clock. The six contestants had been working away in the marquee for hours and were putting their final touches to their show-stopping creations. To Nobby Loveberry's relief, the scene had been one of great merriment and much laughter now that there was no one running interference. And the best thing was that all of their cakes were looking fabulous.

Meanwhile, the front garden had been transformed with reams of bunting and hundreds of balloons. There were already lots of people milling about and setting up their picnic blankets. Clementine gasped at the sight as she and her mother made their way through the throng to the long table around the side of the house that had been reserved for the children's cakes. The turn-out had far exceeded their wildest expectations, so much so that Digby Pertwhistle had already had to extend the table once with Will's help.

Clarissa deposited the cake on the table. 'There,' she said. 'Don't these all look wonderful?'

Clementine wasn't so sure about that. While abundant, the selection of cakes on show was certainly varied. Some looked like what Aunt Violet would call a dog's breakfast, but Clementine knew she wasn't supposed to say that. 'Mhmm,' she replied.

Odette Rousseau hurried over. 'Hello Clarissa, hello Clemmie. I'm afraid Jules has had a little accident. Could I trouble you for a plaster?'

'Of course,' Clarissa said. 'Clemmie, can I leave you to write your name? Don't forget to pop it under your cake, so everyone knows who it belongs to in case it gets chosen.'

In her neatest printing, Clementine wrote her name on the sticky note. She had just finished when Joshua Tribble marched up and flicked her on the arm.

'Ow!' Clementine growled, throwing the boy a fierce look. 'Leave me alone, Joshua.'

'*I'm* going to win,' he said smugly.

Clementine frowned. 'You don't know that.'

'Yes, I do, because my cake is amazing and it's chocolate,' Joshua said, prodding her shoulder.

'Well, mine's chocolate and it's amazing as well,' Clementine retorted. She popped her sticky note under her cake and ran off to join Tilda and Sophie.

Half an hour later, the filming began. Mr and Mrs Loveberry walked around to the front of the house with Pierre dressed in his full baker's uniform. The contestants' cakes were lined up one after the other and the front lawn was covered with picnic blankets and baskets as their family and friends watched on eagerly. Basil was filming everything and even had some cameras in the trees and on the front of the house as well as those being manned by the camera crew. Drew had an extra boom operator stationed out in the garden.

Pierre sampled the cakes and jotted down some notes while the Loveberrys followed him, nodding and smiling. The bakers were all stationed in a line, looking on anxiously as Pierre assessed their creations. There was a tall pink cake covered in the most beautiful hand-made roses, another that looked like a castle complete with turrets and towers and a drawbridge. There was a unicorn cake and one that was square, but when cut open had a colourful checkerboard pattern. Clementine adored one that had a sewing

machine on the top and buttons and fabric around it. She guessed it belonged to Mrs Mogg because the woman was a whiz on a sewing machine and had made dresses for Clementine since she was a baby. The final cake Pierre tasted looked like it was made of asparagus spears, but revealed itself to be a mint-chocolate butter cake inside.

'It gives my wife and I great pleasure to hand over to esteemed baker Pierre Rousseau, who will announce this round's winner for the most show-stopping cake,' Mr Loveberry said.

Mrs Bottomley was fidgeting in the background while Mrs Mogg was smiling, as always. Miss Edwards held on to Mr Moreno's hand. Mr Grimley was laughing at his children, who were turning cartwheels on the lawn. Zander Crowe might even have had a tear in his eye.

'Well,' Pierre began, 'I would first like to congratulate every one of you on the most amazing cakes. These would not be out of place in any fancy patisserie in the country and I would very much like to 'ave them in mine.'

There was a generous round of applause and even some whistling. Then the crowd hushed, waiting for the man's next words.

'The ultimate show-stopper is the very odd and strangely delicious asparagus cake.'

The audience went wild, clapping and cheering. The cake belonged to Tiggy Edwards. Everyone hugged her and she truly beamed. Clementine felt sad that it wasn't Mrs Mogg or Mrs Bottomley, who had worked so hard. It reminded her of the time she and Sophie had missed out on winning the Art prize at school for their papier-mâché pig.

Mr Loveberry smiled and clasped his hands. 'Now we would like to announce the overall winner of the bake-off. This person will receive a cookbook contract and a national publicity tour. We've tallied up the scores from the week's activities and the champion by just one point is . . . Mrs Ethel Bottomley!'

There was a stunned silence. Some of the children even groaned, but Clementine jumped to her feet and clapped loudly. The others soon followed suit. Mrs Bottomley's daughter and grandson charged in to hug the woman, who had fat tears rolling down her cheeks.

Florence Loveberry was standing to the side with a fake smile plastered across her face. She couldn't help but think the woman was a marketing nightmare. They'd have to do something about all that brown before she went on any morning television shows, that was for sure.

'Thank you so much,' Mrs Bottomley said. 'When I was a young woman, I adored baking. That is, until I was put in charge of making a cake for my mother-in-law's birthday party. I thought I'd done a wonderful job, but something had gone awry and the woman declared to everyone at the party that I was the worst baker she'd ever come across. For many years I believed her, but then

I rediscovered my love of baking and these past ten years I've been practising and practising, but never daring to share my creations with anyone. Today, I've proven to myself – and the rest of you who've ever been told you can't – that you can.'

Clementine flashed the woman a huge smile and a big thumbs up.

'Well, congratulations, Mrs Bottomley. I'm sure that your cookbook is going to be a bestseller.' Nobby Loveberry beamed. 'But we have one more job for you before you can celebrate. Will you judge the junior bake-off for us?'

'Ooh, it would be my pleasure,' Ethel said, blowing her nose loudly into a handkerchief. She led the way to the trestle table around the side of the house, and sniffed and prodded and nibbled and nudged before making her decision. It was a chocolate cake that was absolutely perfect in her books.

The children had gathered around, eager to see who had come up trumps.

Ethel Bottomley lifted the plate and pulled out the sticky note. 'The winner is . . .' She paused and narrowed her eyes. 'Joshua Tribble.'

The boy whooped and jumped into the air. 'I won, I won, I won!' he crowed, dancing about on the grass. 'Told you I'd win!'

Frowning, Ethel dipped her finger in the icing and had another taste. She realised what was niggling at her – she had tasted that recipe just the other day. 'Joshua Tribble,' the woman sighed. 'Goodness me. I can't believe that you tried to pass off Clemmie's cake as your own.'

Joshua stamped his foot and folded his arms tightly in front of him. 'But it's my cake. I made that one. Not that other wonky one over there,' he said, gesturing to a similar-looking but rather lopsided chocolate cake.

Clementine's heart was pounding.

'The winner of the junior bake-off is, in fact, Clementine Rose Appleby,' Mrs Bottomley announced.

Much to the great surprise of everyone, Clementine ran to the other side of the trestle table and gave the woman a huge hug.

'Thank you, Mrs Bottomley,' Clementine said. 'I never expected that.'

The woman hugged her right back. 'Me either, Clementine. Me either.'

With filming over for the day, the families and friends went back to enjoying their picnics on the front lawn. A group of children were involved in a spirited game of hide-and-seek, but when Joshua Tribble produced a soccer ball, it was quickly confiscated before any damage could be done.

Clarissa was sitting on the checked picnic rug and eating a honey sandwich, to which she had just added some chicken and pickles. Clementine was sitting opposite her, thinking that was revolting. Drew was finally able to relax and had taken up a spot beside his wife while Uncle Digby popped a champagne cork and was pouring some celebratory drinks for the grown-ups. Will raced over to join the family, having moments before found Teddy hiding behind the woodpile.

'Is there anything left to eat?' the boy panted as he plonked down next to Clementine.

'Mummy,' Clementine said, remembering something the woman had said earlier, 'what is the surprise you have for us?'

Clarissa looked at Drew, whose smile couldn't have been any wider. She pulled the blurry photograph from her pocket. 'So how do you two feel about being a big brother and sister?' Clarissa asked.

Clementine and Will turned and looked at one another. For a second time that day, the children were absolutely stunned.

'Really?' Clementine said, finding her voice.

Will sat up on his knees. 'Is it a boy or a girl?'

Drew chuckled. 'That's a secret for now.'

Aunt Violet rested her head on Digby Pertwhistle's shoulder. 'You do know we're going to be the oldest grandparents in the world,' she said, brushing a tear from her eye.

'And I wouldn't want it any other way,' he replied, squeezing her hand.

Clementine hugged her mother tightly around the middle and placed her ear against her tummy. 'Hello baby,' she whispered, then looked back up at her mother. 'This is not how I thought the holidays would turn out.'

'Oh?' Clarissa said.

Clementine shook her head and grinned. 'No, this is a million times better!'

Cast of Characters

The Appleby household

Clementine Rose Appleby	Six-year-old daughter of Lady Clarissa
Lavender	Clementine's teacup pig
Lady Clarissa Appleby	Clementine's mother and owner of Penberthy House
Digby Pertwhistle	Butler at Penberthy House
Aunt Violet Appleby	Clementine's grandmother
Pharaoh	Aunt Violet's beloved sphynx cat
Drew Barnsley	Clarissa's husband
Will Barnsley	Drew's son

Friends and village folk

Margaret Mogg	Owner of the Penberthy Floss village shop
Clyde Mogg	Margaret Mogg's husband
Claws	Margaret Mogg's tabby cat
Ethel Bottomley	Kindergarten teacher at Ellery Prep
Pierre Rousseau	Owner of Pierre's Patisserie in Highton Mill
Sophie Rousseau	Clementine's best friend
Jules Rousseau	Eight-year-old brother of Sophie
Basil Hobbs	Documentary filmmaker and neighbour
Teddy Hobbs	Six-year-old twin son of Basil and Ana
Tilda Hobbs	Six-year-old twin daughter of Basil and Ana
Joshua Tribble	Clementine's classmate
Astrid	Clever Year One girl
Father Bob	Village minister
Dr Everingham	Doctor at Highton Mill Hospital

Others

Nobby Loveberry	Co-host of *The Great Village Bake-Off*
Florence Loveberry	Co-host of *The Great Village Bake-Off*
Serge Moreno, Tiggy Edwards, Axel Grimley and Zander Crowe	Contestants of *The Great Village Bake-Off*

ABOUT THE AUTHOR

Jacqueline Harvey taught for many years in girls' boarding schools. She is the author of the bestselling Alice-Miranda series and the Clementine Rose series, and was awarded Honour Book in the 2006 Australian CBC Awards for her picture book *The Sound of the Sea*. She now writes full-time and is working on more Alice-Miranda, Clementine Rose, and Kensy and Max adventures.

jacquelineharvey.com.au

Jacqueline Harvey is a passionate educator who enjoys sharing her love of reading and writing with children and adults alike. She is an ambassador for Dymocks Children's Charities and Room to Read. Find out more at dcc.gofundraise.com.au and roomtoread.org.

Look out for Clementine Rose's
next adventure

COMING IN 2019